Max and Lincoln,
this is dedicated to you.

One windy day, Rose and Sammy were playing with their dog Jelly in the meadow down by the river.

As they played, a long, red feather came twirling down right in front of Rose.

She looked to the sky wondering where it came from. Seeing nothing but treetops, she yelled to her little brother, "Hey, look what I found Sammy!" then flicked the feather right under his nose and started to run up the hill. "Come on, let's show it to Mom!"

"Mom, look what we found! What kind of bird has a long, red feather?"

"I don't know," said her mother as she pulled at some weeds in the garden. "Let's go look it up. Maybe it's called a Red-Tailed Farnookler Zwebodi Bird," Mom said.

Rose looked sideways at her Mom. "Farnookler?"

"Just kidding," whispered Mom. "I made that up."

Just before they got to the porch,
Jelly began barking and jumping around
in circles.

Sammy pointed to the back porch
and put his finger to his lips. "Shhh!" he
whispered to Jelly.

There on the railing of the porch was
a beautiful bird with lots of the same red
feathers.

"Hello!" the bird squawked. "Awk! Got any Enchiladas? Awk! Black beans and rice?"

They all looked at each other and then back at the colorful creature.

"Enchiladas?" wondered Mom.

"Hi!" Rose shouted. "Is this yours?" she asked waving the feather around. "What's your name bird?"

"Awk! Clever. My name is Clever. Awk!"

"I'll say," answered Mom with wide eyes.

"Are you a Red-Tailed Farnie Zibodi Bird, like my mother said?" Rose asked.

"Awk! I'm a Macaw, Macaw," he answered.

"So, Clever, where did you come from?" asked Mother.

"Awk! Across the river!" he said. "Across the river!"

Mom shook her head in disbelief. Taking off her sunhat, she asked if the bird would like to be taken home.

"Go home! Awk! Go home!" he cackled.

"Awww," whined the children. "Can't we keep him?"

"Clever might have a family that's missing him," said Mom. "Okay everybody, into the car! Clever, since you're so clever, you sit in the front seat and tell us where to go."

Mom waved everyone into the car as if she were herding a row of ducklings.

"Come on Jelly, you too!" she added, then buckled and snapped and strapped the kids in. Off they went.

They drove toward the bridge that crossed the nearest river. All of a sudden, Clever spoke up. "Awk! Turn around! Go west! Go west!" he repeated.

"But the river is this way," Mom pointed out.

"Awk! Wrong river! Go west! Awk!" came the demand.

"The only river west of here is more than three hours away," Mom said.

"Awk! Go west! Go west!"

"Well guys, what do you think? Are you ready for a long trip? I guess we'll call Dad a little later."

The children cheered happily for the adventure. Jelly barked with delight, and Clever sat calmly in the front seat.

Three hours later they came to another wide river. Tumbling out of the car, Sammy threw sticks for Jelly. Mom stretched while Rose looked for the nearest tree to climb. But Clever didn't get out of the car.

"Clever, are you okay?" Mom asked.
"This _is_ your river, isn't it?"

"Awk! Wrong river! Wrong river! Go
south! Awk! Go south!"

"Come on Jelly!" Rose and Sammy yelled as they all climbed back into the car.

After driving for a bit longer, they decided they would stop for the night. Mom asked what Clever wanted for dinner.

"Awk! Black beans and rice! Awk!"

It took some time to find the special food, but the bird insisted. As they were finishing up, Sammy said, "I wish Dad were here."

"Oh no!" Mom cried out. "We forgot to call Dad!"

The phone only had to ring once
before Dad answered.

"Where are you?!" He yelled so loudly
that Mom had to hold her phone away
from her ear.

Mom explained everything and finally
got Dad to calm down.

The next day, they came to three different rivers, but none of them were Clever's. "Awk! Go south! Go south!" he kept saying.

This went on for days. Whenever Mom asked for the map, Clever would squawk "Go south! Awk! Go south!"

Farther and farther south they drove. Sometimes, in order to get to a river, they would veer off to the east or west. But still none were Clever's river.

At the end of the week, they came to the Rio Grande. Mom stopped the car.

"Map!" she yelled. Four little heads popped up over her shoulder to look at the map with her.

"Well guys, any farther south and we'll be in
Mexico. If we go beyond that, we'll be in Central
America, and then way, way beyond that is
South America. Clever, dare I ask which way?"

Before the bird even got a chance to
answer, the children yelled: "Go south! Go
south!"

"Awk!" Clever nodded his approval.

Continuing south, they drove through
Mexico, then Guatemala, Honduras, Nicaragua,
Costa Rica, Panama, Colombia, and then finally
into Brazil.

"How much farther?" everyone asked
Clever.

"Go south! Awk! Go south!" was the same
answer.

After traveling for many more days,
Mom burst out, "I know where we're going!
It must be the Amazon River! Right Clever?"

Clever bounced happily on the car seat.
"Awk! Right river! Awk! Amazon!"

On and on they drove until one steamy
afternoon, Clever started to flap his wings with joy.
"Turn right! Awk! Turn right!"

"Clever, this isn't a road. It's a path!" Mom said.
But she made the turn and they bumped and jiggled
slowly along.

At the end of the road was a small meadow.
And on the other side of the clearing was the great,
wide Amazon River.

Rose was the first to speak. "I don't want to leave Clever here."

"Me either," Sammy pouted.

"I don't either," Mom said, "but this is Clever's home. He'll be much happier here. Let's just say 'goodbye' and head back to our home."

With long, sad faces, each gave
Clever a hug and a kiss goodbye. Even
Jelly touched noses with Clever.

Clever flew off,
crossing the huge
river while the family
waved goodbye.

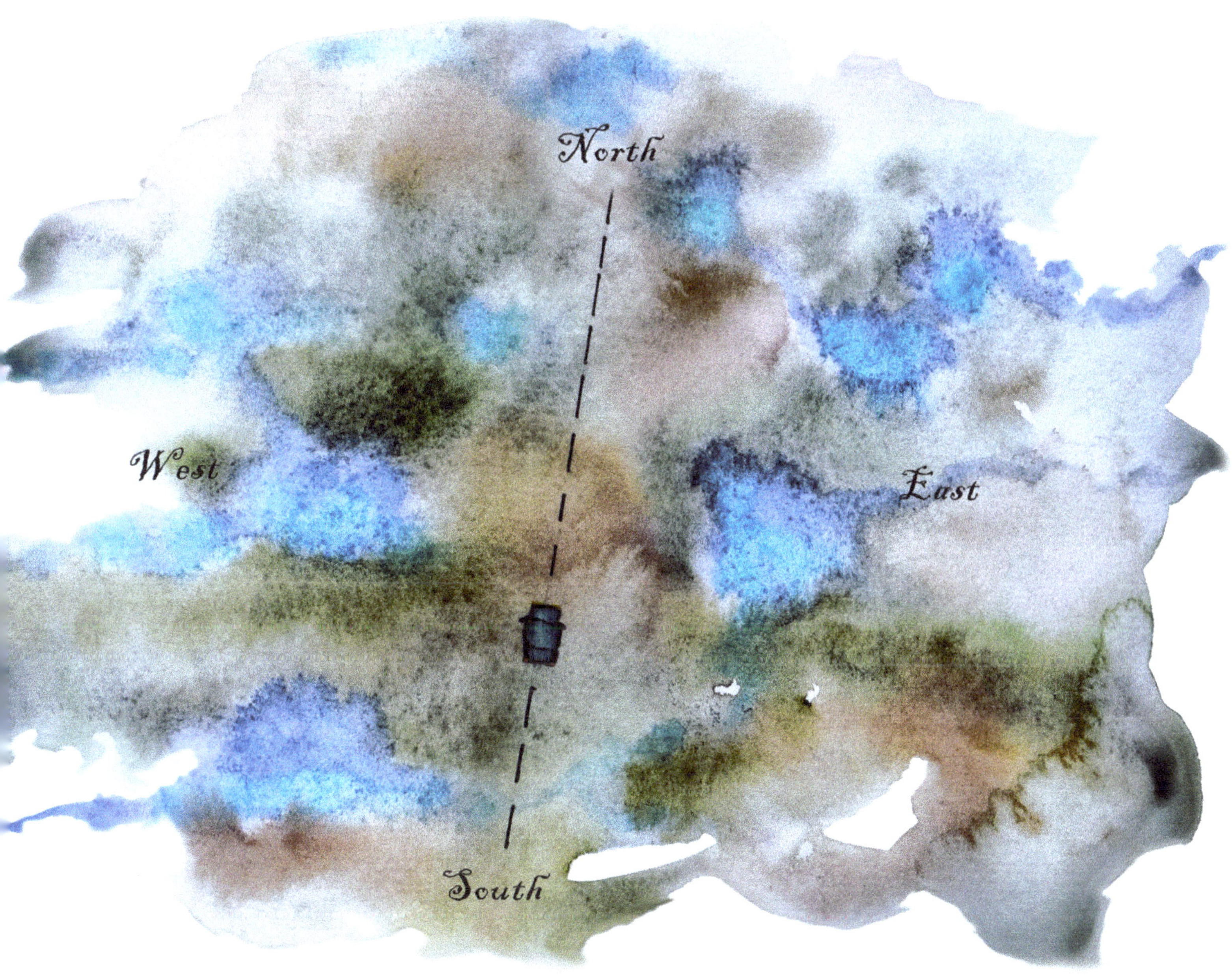

The trip home went a lot faster. They didn't have to stop at each river, and Mom hardly ever yelled for the map. They all missed Dad and were ready to be home.

When they drove up their driveway a few weeks later, they squealed with excitement to see Dad and their little house.

In front of the house, Dad stood waving and yelling.

When they opened the car door, Jelly jumped out and ran up the back steps. He gave a short bark and bounced around in joyful circles.

"Awk! Hello! Hello!" they all heard from the familiar voice. It was Clever! He had somehow beaten them back home!

Rose, Sammy, and Mom stood with their mouths wide open.

"What are you doing here?" Mom asked Clever. "What happened to your family?"

"Awk! You're my family!" squawked Clever.

28

"He came back a few days ago," Dad told everyone. "I've been trying to find food for him while we were waiting for you to come back. But he wouldn't touch birdseed. I even tried tacos and enchiladas like you said. He pecked a little at this and that, but what he kept asking for was egg rolls and fortune cookies. What do you think that means?"

"Road trip!" yelled Rose and Sammy.

Clever nodded and flapped his wings. "Awk! Road trip! Road trip! Awk!"

My thanks to Serena W., Kathy R.,
Leslie S., Ali B., and Danny B. for all
your editing and technical help.

Nick and Lucy,
as always you are my inspiration.